D1448603

Jump, Toad, Jump!

Written by
Ann Bryant

Illustrated by
Gabriele Antonini

Practising long vowel phonemes,
CVCC and CCVC plus polysyllabic words

H46 125 947 9

First published in 2010 by
Franklin Watts
338 Euston Road
London NW1 3BH

Franklin Watts Australia
Hachette Children's Books
Level 17/207 Kent Street
Sydney NSW 2000

Text © Ann Bryant 2010
Illustration © Gabriele Antonini 2010

A CIP catalogue record for this book
is available from the British Library.

ISBN: 978 0 7496 9170 7 (hbk)
ISBN: 978 0 7496 9179 0 (pbk)

Series Editor: Jackie Hamley
Series Advisors: Dr Barrie Wade,
 Dr Hilary Minns
Series Designer: Jonathan Hair

Printed in China

Franklin Watts is a division of
Hachette Children's Books,
an Hachette UK company
www.hachette.co.uk

There is a puzzle at the end of this book.
Here are the answers for you to check later!

The matching words are:
cow bow, brow, how
sheep cheap, creep, sleep
mouse grouse, house, louse
toad code, load, road

Toad had lost his jump.

He was very sad.

3

"Let me help!" said Cow, swishing her tail like a skipping rope. "Now JUMP!"

But it was no good.

Toad just sat still.

"Let me help," said Sheep, tickling Toad with his wool. "Now JUMP!"

8

But Toad just sat still.

"Let me help," said Pig, pushing Toad with his wet snout.

"Get off!" said Toad.

But he did not jump.

"Let me help!" said Donkey.
"Boo!" he shouted, stamping
his hoof.

Toad just sat still.

"It's no good," they all said.
"Sorry, Toad. We think you
have lost your jump."

17

"Wait!" said Mouse.

"Let me help."

"Sorry, Mouse, but if we can't make Toad jump, how can a little mouse do it?" said Sheep.

"I can't," said Mouse,
"but here is ...

"… Elephant!"

"Hello, Toad!" said Elephant.

Toad did a huge jump
right back into his pond.

And so did Cow, Sheep, Pig and Donkey!

29

Puzzle Time!

Match the words that rhyme
to the pictures.

cow

sleep

house

road

bow

sheep

code

louse

mouse

how

creep

load

grouse

toad

brow

cheap

See page 2 for answers.

Notes for parents and teachers

READING CORNER PHONICS has been structured to provide maximum support for children learning to read through synthetic phonics. The stories are designed for independent reading but may also be used by adults for sharing with young children.

The teaching of early reading through synthetic phonics focuses on the 44 sounds in the English language, and how these sounds correspond to their written form in the 26 letters of the alphabet. Carefully controlled vocabulary makes these books accessible for children at different stages of phonics teaching, progressing from simple CVC (consonant-vowel-consonant) words such as "top" (t-o-p) to trisyllabic words such as "messenger" (mess-en-ger). READING CORNER PHONICS allows children to read words in context, and also provides visual clues and repetition to further support their reading. These books will help develop the all important confidence in the new reader, and encourage a love of reading that will last a lifetime!

If you are reading this book with a child, here are a few tips:

1. Talk about the story before you start reading. Look at the cover and the title. What might the story be about? Why might the child like it?

2. Encourage the child to reread the story, and to retell the story in their own words, using the illustrations to remind them what has happened.

3. Discuss the story and see if the child can relate it to their own experience, or perhaps compare it to another story they know.

4. Give praise! Small mistakes need not always be corrected. If a child is stuck on a word, ask them to try and sound it out and then blend it together again, or model this yourself. For example "wish" w-i-sh "wish".

READING CORNER PHONICS covers two grades of synthetic phonics teaching, with three levels at each grade. Each level has a certain number of words per story, indicated by the number of bars on the spine of the book:

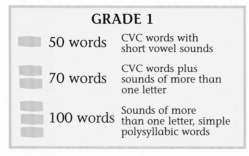

GRADE 1	
50 words	CVC words with short vowel sounds
70 words	CVC words plus sounds of more than one letter
100 words	Sounds of more than one letter, simple polysyllabic words

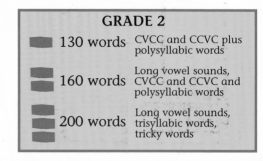

GRADE 2	
130 words	CVCC and CCVC plus polysyllabic words
160 words	Long vowel sounds, CVCC and CCVC and polysyllabic words
200 words	Long vowel sounds, trisyllabic words, tricky words